How the Elephant Got His Trunk

Written by Lou Kuenzler
Illustrated by Alberto Arzeni

Collins

When elephants didn't have trunks, long ago,
Eddie the elephant wanted to know …

4

Why is Giraffe so tall and spotty?

Eddie's questions drove everyone potty.

5

Eddie always asked things like
"Who? What? When?"
But the animals ignored him
again and again.

6

What does a crocodile have for his tea?

No one replied ... so he went off to see.

Down by the great,
green, greasy river,
he saw something slip
and slide and slither.

Eddie strode on down the long river bank.

What is that great,
green, greasy plank?

Croc grabbed Eddie's nose
with a mighty SNAP!

Led go please! Led go!
You're hurtig be.

13

Stretching and straining … Eddie jumped ashore.

14

But Croc held on tight with his toothy jaw.

15

Snake slithered down to help Eddie out.

PING! Croc let go of the rubbery snout.

Eddie's new nose made him proud.

Now I can trumpet really loud!

No one could ignore the elephant now.
He kept trumpeting questions:
"Who? What? When? How?"

20

Of course, every elephant has a trunk now.
And this story told you exactly how!

From small nose to long trunk

🐾 Ideas for reading 🐾

Written by Gillian Howell
Primary Literacy Consultant

Reading objectives:
- discuss the significance of the title and events
- read words with contractions, and understand that the apostrophe represents the omitted letter(s)
- learn to appreciate rhymes and poems
- make inferences on the basis of what is being said and done

Spoken language objectives:
- give well-structured descriptions, explanations and narratives for different purposes, including for expressing feelings
- participate in discussions and role play
- use spoken language to develop understanding through speculating, imagining and exploring ideas

Curriculum links: Art, Geography

Interest words: elephant, trunk, ostrich, giraffe, crocodile, greasy, slither, curious

Word count: 239 words

Resources: pens, paper, art materials

Build a context for reading

This book can be read over two or more reading sessions.

- Read the title and look together at the cover illustration. Ask the children if they can name any of the animals in the picture.
- Ask the children if they have read any stories about how animals got their features, e.g. how the camel got his hump. Establish that this is a traditional tale and ask them to predict what the story will be about.
- Turn to the back cover and read the blurb to confirm the children's ideas.